The Bunny With the Basket© and the Golden Egg

Written by Jennifer Diehl, Shauna Murray & Lisa Rettino

Illustrated by Brian Meulener

Photos by Laura Bruen.

Third Edition: 2016

ISBN #: 978-0-9915325-0-6

www.bunnywiththebasket.com

Manufactured in Shenzhen, China through Asia Pacific Offset.
11/2016
11272016
This product conforms to CPSIA 2008.

Dear Family,

While celebrating Christmas Eve with one another, we discussed the next holiday we looked forward to. We realized that while our Easter Traditions varied, our message was the same. Taking into account each of our customs, a wonderful tradition was born.

In this special tradition the Easter Bunny has helpers who are each called the "Bunny with the Basket." Approximately 12 days before Easter, the Bunny with the Basket arrives holding a mini basket and in it is a golden egg! The golden egg contains a special note from the Easter Bunny, and the children enthusiastically write back. Once they are fast asleep, the Bunny with the Basket delivers their message to the Easter Bunny. This interaction goes on each day leading up to Easter. The kids can't wait for Easter morning because they know that if their Bunny with the Basket reports their good behavior the Easter Bunny will reward them with a basket of goodies. Each spring the children look forward to the arrival of their Bunny with the Basket.

Introduce the art of letter writing to your children, with the help of *Bunny with the Basket.* Our collective girls' (as we each have two) thoroughly enjoy this tradition, and we hope they continue to for years to come. Our hope is that you will enjoy it as much as we do. It's educational, interactive, and a ton of fun!

Best Wishes and Happy Easter!

Jennifer, Lisa & Shauna

Sign up at www.bunnywiththebasket.com
to receive special notes from The Easter Bunny every Spring!

Each year after Christmas when he's all done with wish lists, Santa has one last important thing to do...

Every child knows
about Santa Claus and the Easter Bunny,
but did you know that they're good friends?
Each year they get together,
as soon as Christmas ends.

NICE

Sabina Superstar
Logan Loviley
Anna Awesome
Kiley Kindhearted
Laney Lovebug
Cary Caresalot

Katelyn Kissable
Sydney Sassie
Lily Loveable
Kate Captivate
Nicholas Neat
Erin Irresistible

Garrett Gregarious
Luke Limitless
Connor Crafty
Patrick Precious
Lauren Lively
Hank Handsomely
Alex Angel

Sadie Sweetie
Dakota Dynamite
Jaiden Genius
Christopher Caring
Kayla Courteous
Loredana Listener
Blake Bravery

NAUGHTY

Santa shares all
of his naughty and nice notes
from the past Christmas season.
The Easter Bunny listens closely,
as Santa explains each reason.

When the Easter Bunny returns home,
there's loads of work to do.

Santa has his elves,
and the Easter Bunny has helpers too!
We are his Bunnies with the Baskets
and have a Golden Egg for you!

Every Bunny gets a family
of his or her very own.

Then we pack up our eggs and baskets,
and hop off to your home.

Hippity Hop!
Congrats to you,
you've been chosen
to visit the
Lafferty 2!
Watch over the tots
and report back to me.
Together we'll make Easter
as Great as can be!
Best of luck,
E.B.

I am your very own Bunny with the Basket
and this is what I do...

Twelve days before Easter
I hop down the bunny trail,
on my way to you!

I arrive at your home
after everyone's asleep.
I'll be very, very quiet
and will not make a peep.

On my very first night
I must find the perfect spot,
from where I can watch over
each little tot.

Once you have found me,
please give me a name.
Maybe something sweet or silly,
like Snowflake, Fluffy
or even Billy.

And please do not touch me
or move me around,
I'm happy in the cozy spot I found.

Next you will search
for the egg made of gold!
Where will you find it?
What will it hold?

Now it's your turn.

Take time to write back.

Draw me a picture, or pack me a snack!

And don't forget to place the egg back in my basket.

Dear Easter Buny,
We Hav Bin
Good this year.

Each night when you're sleeping
and the moon is bright,
I hop back to Easter Village
with the Golden Egg
held tight.

The Easter Bunny
will love what you wrote,
and he will reply once again with a note.
Or maybe he will reply with a treat,
perhaps a jellybean or something sweet.

I'll hide your egg in a
new spot each day.

Where will I hide it
you just never know.
When you awake in the morning
on an egg hunt you'll go.

What will the message inside the egg say?
"Good job with your homework!",
or
"Well done cleaning your room!",
or it might say,
"Share with your sister and
don't make her boo hoo."

Whatever it says you must take it to heart
– and if you do,
you will find a special Easter Basket
on Easter Day just for you!

When Easter is over, I'll return to Easter Village
where I'll stay until next year.

Here's one last thing that is very important,
and you will want to hear...

The Easter Bunny keeps a book of notes—
notes on all of you!
And guess who comes to my backyard
to discuss them and review?
Well Santa Claus of course…
and all his reindeer too!

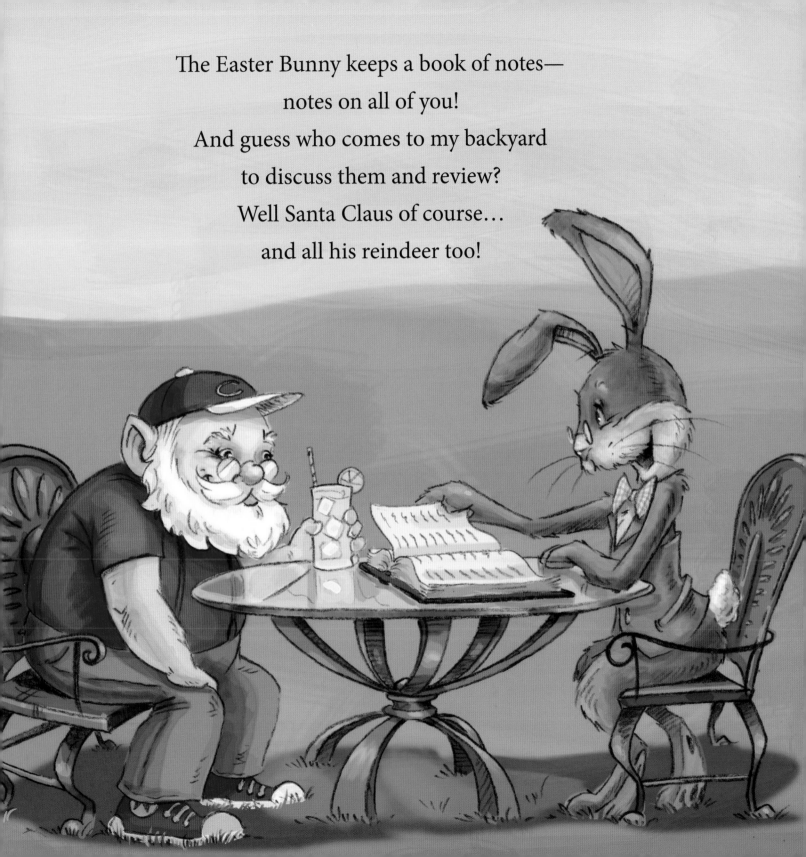

Thanks for the fun,
and a great Easter season.
I'll see you next year
for the very same reason.

The End

About The Authors

From left to right: J. Diehl, S. Murray, L. Rettino

Jennifer Diehl is a graduate of William Patterson University where she earned her bachelor's degree in education and communications. She is a former teacher and presently involved in volunteer work for a number of organizations such as The Foundation to Save the Jersey Shore, Monmouth Park Charity Fund, and The Junior League, just to name a few. Jennifer resides with her husband, Tim, and daughters Jaiden and Dakota, in Rumson, NJ

Shauna Murray is an alumna of California State University, San Bernardino. She is a professional in the insurance and financial service industry. She is dedicated to raising her daughters and is active in volunteerism at their school. Shauna, her husband, Thomas, and daughters Sabina and Anna reside in Rumson, NJ.

Lisa Rettino is a graduate of Iona College where she earned a bachelor's degree in marketing, and a graduate of Baruch College where she earned an MBA. She is a former pharmaceutical advertising executive and currently is a free-lance account person. She spends her free time volunteering at her daughters' elementary school. Lisa, her husband, Lou, and daughters Logan and Sydney reside in Rumson, NJ.

Brian Meulener is a general dentist in Little Silver, NJ. He received his DMD from Rutgers School of Dental Medicine. Brian also has a Bachelor of Fine Arts from the University of Delaware, and a Master of Fine Arts from the School of Visual Arts in NYC. He worked as a freelance artist/illustrator, interior designer, and art director. Brian, his wife, Kristin, and daughters Lily and Kate reside in Little Silver, NJ.